Don't Forget the Knight Light

by Tina Gagliardi   illustrated by Patrick Girouard

Carly's DRAGON DAYS

magic wagon

visit us at www.abdopublishing.com

Published by Magic Wagon, a division of the ABDO Group, 8000 West 78th Street, Edina, Minnesota 55439. Copyright © 2009 by Abdo Consulting Group, Inc. International copyrights reserved in all countries. All rights reserved. No part of this book may be reproduced in any form without written permission from the publisher.

Looking Glass Library™ is a trademark and logo of Magic Wagon.

Printed in the United States.

Text by Tina Gagliardi
Illustrations by Patrick Girouard
Edited by Nadia Higgins and Jill Sherman
Interior layout and design by Nicole Brecke
Cover design by Nicole Brecke

Library of Congress Cataloging-in-Publication Data

Gagliardi, Tina.
  Don't forget the knight light / by Tina Gagliardi ; illustrated by Patrick Girouard.
      p. cm. — (Carly's dragon days)
  ISBN 978-1-60270-593-7
  [1. Dragons—Fiction.] I. Girouard, Patrick, ill. II. Title.
  PZ7.G1242Don 2009
  [E]—dc22
                              2008035950

At recess, the third graders huddled together. None of them had ever been to the museum.

"My brother says the room with the knight suits is really scary," Randy said.

"I heard that too!" Lily said.

Abigail snorted. "You guys are such scaredy-frogs!"

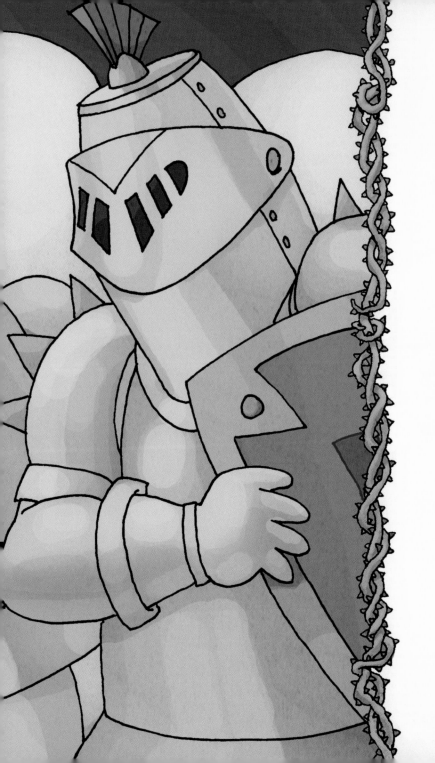

At dinner, Carly could only think about knights, knights, knights. She heard they were super-huge humans. Their swords could slice right through dragon scales!

Carly pushed her plate away. She was way too scared to eat.

That night, Carly couldn't sleep.

"Gretchen?" she called to her imaginary human friend.

Gretchen appeared right away. "Yes?"

"Do you think the knights will really be scary?" Carly asked.

"I hope not!" Gretchen said.

Just then, Carly heard clinking. Gretchen saw something shiny in the closet.

"Mooooommmmmmy!" Carly shouted.

Carly's mom came running. "What is it, honey?"

"There's a knight in my closet!"

Carly's mother opened the closet. "See?" she said. "No knights."

But Carly wasn't sure. It seemed that knights were hiding everywhere.

"Gretchen sees them too," Carly said.

"Oh, you and your imagination," Carly's mom said, patting her on her head.

Carly's mom turned to leave.

"Mom, WAIT!" Carly howled. "There's another noise coming from my desk!"

Her mother sighed. She checked under the desk. She opened the drawers. "There's nothing there. See?" she said.

Carly's mom looked at her frightened daughter. Carly's skin was as pale as a lizard's belly.

"Hang on. I'll be right back," said her mother as she left.

Carly's mother came with a tiny dragon statue. "Here's a night light for you," she said.

"A KNIGHT light?" asked Carly. "Does it really scare knights away?"

Her mother realized Carly's mistake. But it gave her a good idea. "Yes," she said, "this special light makes knights stay away."

Carly's mom plugged in the light. The scary shadows went away. At last, Carly fell asleep.

The next day in class, Lily had more scary news about the Knight Room.

"My sister said that if you are the last dragon there, the knights will come to life and eat you up!" she said.

Finally, the day of the field trip arrived. Carly and Lily sat together on the bus.

Lily saw Carly playing with something in her book bag.

"What do you have?" Lily asked.

"My knight light," Carly replied. She explained all about its special powers.

"Can I hold it?" Lily asked.

"OK," Carly said. "But just for a second."

Just as Carly was handing the light to Lily, Abigail's arm shot between them.

"Let me see!" Abigail said.

"No way!" Lily said. She grabbed for the light.

"Abigail! Lily! No!" Carly shouted. But it was too late. The light dropped. It shattered everywhere.

Carly hugged her stomach. "I think I'm going to be sick," she said. But it was too late to have a sick day.

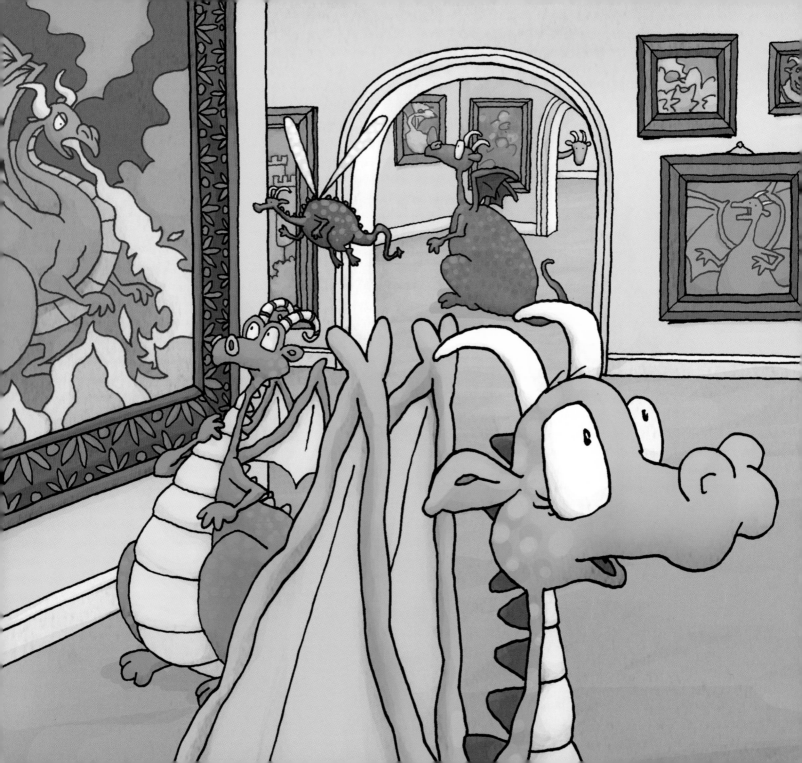

At the museum, Carly tried to admire the cool dragon statues. She tried to be amazed by the burning castle. She made an effort to take part in the hidden treasure game.

But it was no use. All she could think about was knights, knights, knights.

At last, the class approached the Knight Room. Carly's feet felt frozen in place. From the door, she watched her classmates inside the room.

"What's the big deal about a bunch of imaginary humans?" she heard Abigail say.

"Imaginary humans!" The words made Carly's feet unfreeze. "Gretchen!" Carly called. Her best friend showed up right away. Together, they went in.

Carly and Gretchen had so much fun, they didn't even notice when Carly's classmates left.

Finally, Carly noticed she was the only dragon in the room! Would the knights come to life?

Just then, Gretchen poked her head inside a knight helmet and laughed. That made Carly laugh, too.

Carly didn't need a knight light after all.

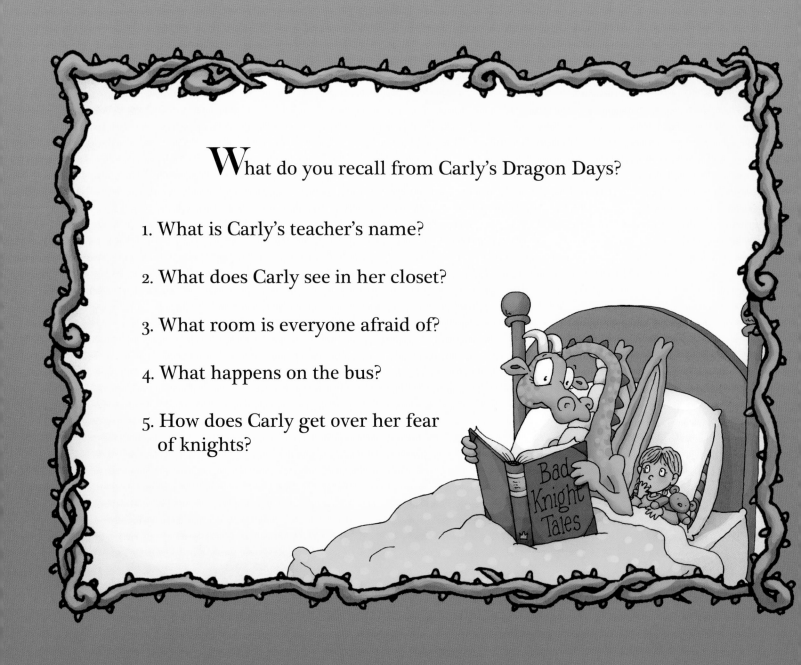

What do you recall from Carly's Dragon Days?

1. What is Carly's teacher's name?

2. What does Carly see in her closet?

3. What room is everyone afraid of?

4. What happens on the bus?

5. How does Carly get over her fear of knights?